Dear Parent:
Your child's love of reading starts here!

P9-BYK-917

Every child learns to read in a different way and at his or her own speed. Some go back and forth between reading levels and read favorite books again and again. Others read through each level in order. You can help your young reader improve and become more confident by encouraging his or her own interests and abilities. From books your child reads with you to the first books he or she reads alone, there are I Can Read Books for every stage of reading:

SHARED READING
Basic language, word repetition, and whimsical illustrations, ideal for sharing with your emergent reader

BEGINNING READING
Short sentences, familiar words, and simple concepts for children eager to read on their own

READING WITH HELP
Engaging stories, longer sentences, and language play for developing readers

READING ALONE
Complex plots, challenging vocabulary, and high-interest topics for the independent reader

ADVANCED READING
Short paragraphs, chapters, and exciting themes for the perfect bridge to chapter books

I Can Read Books have introduced children to the joy of reading since 1957. Featuring award-winning authors and illustrators and a fabulous cast of beloved characters, I Can Read Books set the standard for beginning readers.

A lifetime of discovery begins with the magical words "I Can Read!"

Visit www.icanread.com for information on enriching your child's reading experience.

HarperCollins®, 🐻®, and I Can Read Book® are trademarks of HarperCollins Publishers.

The Berenstain Bears' Class Trip. Copyright © 2009 by Berenstain Bears, Inc. All rights reserved. Manufactured in China. No part of this book may be used or reproduced in any manner whatsoever without written permission except in the case of brief quotations embodied in critical articles and reviews. For information address HarperCollins Children's Books, a division of HarperCollins Publishers, 195 Broadway, New York, NY 10007. www.icanread.com

Library of Congress catalog card number: 2008935356
ISBN 978-0-06-168973-4 (trade bdg.)—ISBN 978-0-06-057416-1 (pbk.)
15 16 SCP 10 9 8 7 6 5 4
❖
First Edition

I Can Read!™

BEGINNING 1 READING

The Berenstain Bears'
Class Trip

Jan & Mike Berenstain

HarperCollinsPublishers

Brother Bear's class is going on a trip.

The class is going to a honey farm.

Mama and Papa Bear are

teacher's helpers on the trip.

"Mmm," says Papa Bear, licking his lips.

"I hope they give out free samples."

"I am sure they do," says Mama Bear.

Sister Bear is going, too.

There is an extra seat on the bus

next to Teacher Bob.

Honey Bear will stay at home

with Gramps and Gran.

The bus is on its way.

"Let's all sing!" says Cousin Fred.

"Ninety-nine jars of honey on the wall . . ."

sings the class.

Papa Bear joins in.

"Are we almost there?" asks Sister.

"Almost!" answers Papa.

They see a sign:

BEAR COUNTRY HONEY FARM, NEXT EXIT.

"Hooray!" yells the class.

Brother Bear sniffs the air.

"Smell that?" he says. "Honey!"

They all take a deep breath.

"*Mmm!*" They sigh.

"I can almost taste that honey now,"
says Papa, licking his lips again.
"Look! We are here!" says Sister.

They all get off the bus.

Teacher Bob leads the way.

They scc a huge field of beehives.

The sound of buzzing bees fills the air.

"Over there is the clover field,"

says Teacher Bob.

"Thousands of bees gather nectar there.

They bring it back to the hives

and make it into honey."

"How do they do that?" asks Brother.

"Look," says Teacher Bob.

He points to a hive.

"You can see for yourself."

One of the hives has a glass side.

The cubs can see the bees making honey.

"See that big bee?" says Papa.

"That is the queen."

"Correct," says Teacher Bob.

"All the others are her children."

"Wow," says Sister.

"She has more children

than the Old Bear in the Shoe!"

"How do you get the honey

out of the hive?" asks Brother.

"I'll show you," says Papa.

He lifts the lid of a hive.

"No! No!" says Teacher Bob.

A huge cloud of bees flies out.

"Follow me!" shouts Teacher Bob.

All the bears run into the honey barn.

Teacher Bob slams the door shut
just in time.

"Now you will see the correct way
to get the honey out," he says.

The cubs look out the window.
Beekeepers are gathering honey.
They wear special suits and hats
to keep from getting stung.

First, the beekeepers blow smoke into
the hives to make the bees sleepy.
Then they lift out the honeycombs.

They bring the honeycombs into the barn.

They put them on a big wheel.

They turn the crank.

Golden honey pours into a big vat.

Papa cannot wait to taste the honey.

He leans over too far and gets

honcy all over himself.

"While Papa Bear is getting cleaned up, you may all have some honey samples," says Teacher Bob.

"Yea!" cry the cubs.

29

The class is back on the bus
heading home.
Mama Bear says, "I saved a honey
sample for you, Papa dear."

"No, thank you," says Papa.

"I have already had my sample!"